Rainbow Days

The Gold Bowl

Written by
Valerie Bolling

Art by
Kai Robinson

ACORN™
SCHOLASTIC INC.

For my nieces, Anyah and Zorah, who provided the inspiration
for Zoya's character and her name. May all in your lives glitter!
—**VB**

To Jay
—**KR**

Text copyright © 2023 by Valerie Bolling
Illustrations copyright © 2023 by Kai Robinson

Library of Congress Cataloging-in-Publication Data

Names: Bolling, Valerie, author. | Robinson, Kai (Illustrator), illustrator.
Title: The gold bowl / written by Valerie Bolling; illustrated by Kai Robinson.
Description: First edition. | New York: Acorn/Scholastic, Inc., 2023. |
Series: Rainbow days; 2 | Audience: Ages 4–6. | Audience: Grades K–1. |
Summary: Zoya wants to give her dog Coco a birthday present, and with
her mother's help finally settles on painting his bowl gold, with lots of glitter.
Identifiers: LCCN 2022023169 (print) | ISBN 9781338805963 (paperback) |
ISBN 9781338805970 (library binding)
Subjects: LCSH: Dogs—Juvenile fiction. | Birthdays—Juvenile fiction. |
Gifts—Juvenile fiction. | Painting—Juvenile fiction. | CYAC:
Dogs—Fiction. | Birthdays—Fiction. | Gifts—Fiction. |
Painting—Fiction. | LCGFT: Fiction.
Classification: LCC PZ7.1.B656 Go 2023 (print) |
DDC 813.6 [E]—dc23/eng/20220823
LC record available at https://lccn.loc.gov/2022023169

10 9 8 7 6 5 4 3 2 1   23 24 25 26 27

Printed in China   62
First edition, September 2023
Edited by Katie Carella
Book design by Jaime Lucero

Necklace

My name is Zoya.

I love to make art.

My puppy is my best friend.
His name is Coco. He makes art, too!

Today is Coco's birthday.
I will make a gift for my pup!

I will make a necklace! I grab yarn.

I twist and loop the yarn.

The yarn slips. I try again. And again.

I will make something else for Coco.

Oh! Oh! I know!

I will make Coco's treats look pretty.

I grab white frosting and two plates.

I put frosting on each plate.

Drip, drip. I add one color to each plate.

I frost the treats. I brush and dot them.

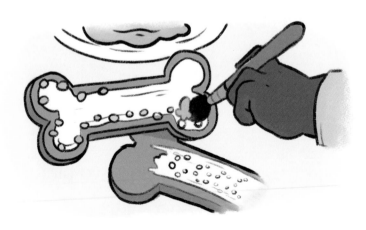

The treats look perfect!

"Mom, come see what I made for Coco," I say.

"Those treats look pretty," Mom says.
"But Coco cannot eat that frosting."

Now what? No yarn necklace. No frosted treats.
What can I make? Oh! Oh! I know!

Coco's bowl needs color! I will paint it.
That will be my gift for Coco!

Bowl

I cannot wait to make Coco's gift.
I will paint his bowl. Coco will like that!

What color will Coco like?

Does he have a favorite color?

Coco's toy is blue.

His leash is green. His bed is red.

Coco wins first prize for being the best pup.
So his gift should look like a prize!

I will paint Coco's bowl gold.
I grab my gold paint.

Swish, swish.

I paint until the bowl shines like the sun.

I wait for the bowl to dry.

"Mom, come see what I made for Coco," I say.

"Coco's bowl looks pretty," Mom says.
"But that paint will wash off."

Mom cleans Coco's bowl to show me.
I watch the paint run down the drain.

Mom squeezes special paint onto a plate.
Paint comes out of the tube like toothpaste.

I dip my brush into the paint.
I swish it around.

I take my time.

This gift must be perfect for Coco.

I am done.
I wait for the bowl to dry.

Coco's gift will be ready soon.

I am happy. I want Coco to be happy, too.

I hope he will like eating out of his gold bowl.
I hope I have made the perfect gift for Coco!

Coco's gift is almost ready.
I cannot wait to give it to him!

I painted Coco's bowl gold.

There is one more step.

Mom squeezes clear paint onto a plate.
She says, "This will make the gold paint shine."

When Mom says "shine," Coco wags his tail.
Coco likes things that shine.

I am glad Coco's bowl will shine.
But something is missing.

Oh! Oh! I know!
Coco's bowl needs glitter!

Coco brings the glitter.
It is green. The glitter matches his leash!

Swoosh! Glitter makes everything better.

I sprinkle the green glitter into the clear paint.

Next, I grab blue glitter to match Coco's toy.
Then I grab red to match Coco's bed.

I need one more color.
What color should I pick?

Silver will make the other colors shine.

Coco brings the glitter.

Swoosh! I add blue, red, and silver.
I swirl all four colors with my paintbrush.

Swish, swish. I paint Coco's bowl.
The glitter twinkles like stars.

Coco's bowl needs one more thing.
I grab my black paint.

Coco adds a paw print that looks like a heart.

We wait for the gold bowl to dry.

Coco barks. I know what he wants!
I put a treat in the bowl. Coco eats it!

I am happy Coco likes his gift.
"Happy Birthday, Coco!" I say.